# 'Night, Farm

Library of Congress Cataloging-in-Publication Data

Carmi, Giora.
'Night, farm / written and illustrated by Giora Carmi.
p.    cm.
"A Calico book."
Summary: A child at bedtime bids goodnight to the cornfield,
tractor, chickens, and other parts of life on the farm.
ISBN 0-8092-4352-0
[1. Bedtime—Fiction.    2. Farm life—Fiction.]    I. Title.
PZ7.K1425Ni    1989
[E]—dc19                                      88-36796
                                               CIP
                                               AC

Published by Contemporary Books, Inc.
180 North Michigan Avenue, Chicago, Illinois 60601
Library of Congress Catalog Card Number: 88-36796
International Standard Book Number: 0-8092-4352-0
Manufactured in the United States of America

Published simultaneously in Canada by Beaverbooks, Ltd.
195 Allstate Parkway, Valleywood Business Park
Markham, Ontario L3R 4T8 Canada

# 'Night, Farm

*Written and Illustrated by*

### GIORA CARMI

## A CALICO BOOK

Published by Contemporary Books, Inc.

CHICAGO · NEW YORK

# 'Night, Cornfield

★

# 'Night, Tractor

# 'Night, Milk Cows

# 'Night, Barn

# 'Night, Chickens

# 'Night, Dog

# 'Night, Porch Swing

*'Night, Kittens*

*'Night, Farm*